PLATYPUS TALES:

a quartet of short stories

celebrating

the delightfully odd

from four BC writers

Lintusen Press

Presents

PLATYPUS TALES:

a quartet of short stories
celebrating
the delightfully odd

from four BC writers

LINTUSEN PRESS

About this book

The platypus is so odd that in 1799 the British naturalist examining the first specimen of these Australian creatures presumed it was a hoax.

Consider the platypus
- duck bill
- otter body
- venomous males
- no stomach
- lays eggs
- lactates
- glows under black light
- has electroreception

So many unexpected elements merged!
What a delightful oddity is a platypus!

In each of these four stories the reader confronts oddities and the delightfully unexpected. Each story features a metaphorical platypus, whether the beast is mentioned or not. Come delight in the odd and unexpected.

Finnian Burnett

Finnian Burnett's work explores the intersections of the human body, mental health, and gender identity. They are a recipient of a Canada Council for the Arts grant, a finalist in the 2023 CBC nonfiction prize, and a 2024 Pushcart nominee. Their flash fiction collection, *The Price of Cookies*, is available through Off Topic Publishing. When not writing or teaching, Finnian enjoys walking, *Star Trek*, and cat memes. Finnian can be found at www.finnburnett.com

Rock Dangerfield Flew Away

Finnian Burnett

ROCK DANGERFIELD COULD HAVE been an actor, an adventurer, a world-renowned zoologist. His mother, who spent her pregnancy watching Marlon Perkins and David Attenborough explore the wild natural world, insisted on a power name, put her foot down about it over her husband's protest.

Elbert Dangerfield, Rock's father, very much wanted to name their son "Clarence," after Elbert's father.

But Rock's mother, Vanessa, envisioned her son leading the life she had always wanted. Her son was going to be an explorer—perhaps in the wildest parts of the world. Maybe he'd discover a new species, or perhaps he'd become the world's foremost expert on platypuses. She would travel with him to exotic locales, perhaps he would lead a group of researchers on a jungle journey, and she would wait at a resort for them all to return. *You only have one life,* she used to tell him. *Don't squander it.*

Vanessa and Rock spent hours pouring over animal books and watching nature documentaries. Rock's bedroom, lined with posters of lizards, leopards, and strange spiders or bugs Vanessa couldn't identify, became home for hamsters, abandoned cats, and one fluffy chinchilla a neighbour with a penchant for exotic animals bought and then discarded.

Rock could have been the next host of Wild America, the world's greatest adventurer, the new Jack Hanna. *You only have one life,* Vanessa would say, squeezing Rock's hand. *Live it.*

Rock could have been any of those things, but he wasn't. On her early death bed, when Rock was just sixteen, Vanessa knew Rock was destined for an office job, not adventures. Without her to guide him, how would her introverted son break out and become what he was meant to be?

After his mother died, Rock turned inward. He spent time with his animals, dragged himself to school. *Get a job,* his father told him at graduation. *Something to secure your future.*

Don't go chasing dreams, his dad said one day, tearing down the pictures from Rock's bedroom walls.

Rock watched his favorite picture of a paddle of platypuses being ripped to shreds, a rare picture indeed because the platypus is a solitary creature, just like him, and also kind of ugly and awkward, just like him. *You only have one life*, he heard his mother saying. But he pushed it away.

Be an accountant, his dad said, and Rock became an accountant. Not a rich one, to be sure, but an honest one. He worked in the county accounting department and, though he was on salary, he brought reports home with him to finish at night without hope of overtime pay.

A solid worker, his boss wrote on his annual reviews. *Comes in on time. Works late. Doesn't take long lunches.*

Solid and dependable, but Peter Mayberry, who often came in late and who had had an affair with the mayor's ex-wife, got the promotions. So many promotions, in fact, he became Rock's boss and when budget cuts came, Peter said, *I'm so sorry, Rock. So very sorry.*

Rock stood in the queue for unemployment, holding his resume in his hand. *One job*, the clerk said. *Since 1993.* She paused to shake her head. *Is there anything else you can do?* She asked, compassion briefly skittering across her face.

I like platypuses, Rock replied.

Platypi, the clerk said, and she stamped his papers and told him to come back next week.

His father, who worked for the same company his entire life and retired with a gold watch and a perfect attendance certificate, told him to go see a job counselor.

Rock found one on Yelp who had mixed reviews. But he went to the counselor and the woman made him paint large swathes of colour on poster board and paste clippings from magazines across it.

What is your passion? the counselor asked him, and Rock said, *I like platypuses.*

Isn't it platypi? the counselor said, but she rolled up his collage and told him to take it home and meditate on it. *It isn't too late to follow your dreams*, she said.

Rock plastered the collage to his wall, the first thing he'd hung since his father tore down his posters long ago. He rifled through his drawers, found a picture of his mother. She stood in the basket of a hot air balloon, her hair wrapped in a kerchief. Smiling, holding a glass of champagne. Rock's father was not in the picture, literally or figuratively.

Rock called his dad. *I'm going on a trip.*

No, his father replied. *Don't squander your*

savings. Get another job.

So, Rock tried. He made the rounds from the unemployment office to the job counselor. He crafted resumes and walked downtown, handing them to every office. And in his head, his mother's voice, always. *You have one life, Rock.*

He finally got an interview in one of the offices downtown. They brought him coffee and he sat with three people in suits. They asked him what he brought to the company, and he answered in all the ways the clerk at the unemployment office told him to answer.

It would be a good job, Rock thought. Decent pay, retirement plan. And he'd have dental insurance and a prescription plan and a good salary and though sometimes he might have to take work home, it wouldn't take him long to work smarter.

What is your passion? They asked.

Platypuses, Rock said in his head, and his mother's voice, *one life, Rock, one valuable life.*

I just want to do a good job, Rock answered. *I want to serve the company.*

Welcome aboard, they said and stood to shake his hand.

But Rock was shaking, too, his hands trembling, his heart pounding. *I can't do this*, he said, and he spun, dropping the coffee as he ran.

And Rock lived on his unemployment cheques, and he watched YouTube videos, and he took classes. He weaved fibres of rattan and hemp, creating a basket big enough for himself and a friend, some sandwiches, a bottle of Cheval Blanc 1947, and of course, an opener and two glasses because Rock was always prepared. He spent his off days haunting the hot air balloon field where Harold, the proprietor taught him everything he could.

And one day, Rock loaded the basket into a rented truck and drove to the hot air balloon service where Harold waited, and while the attendants hooked the balloon to the basket, Harold and Rock took a walk.

Are you sure you want to do this, Harold said.

So sure, Rock told him.

Harold, who was recently divorced and ready for a change, let the back of his hand brush against Rock's hand. And the two men smiled.

Where are we going then? Harold asked.

We're going to Australia, Rock said as they approached the basket where the attendants were finishing the pre-flight checks. *I'm going to see platypuses.*

Aren't they called platypi? One of the attendants

said.

Rock ignored him. Harold helped him into the basket and jumped in after. Harold even let Rock turn on the flame.

Rock stared over the side as they took air.

And Rock was floating, patting his front pocket where his mother's photograph lived and *this was it*, he thought, *this could be the end*. He didn't know what he was doing, not really. He didn't know if they could get across an ocean, didn't even really understand why he hadn't just bought a plane ticket and flown to Australia and just gone to a damn zoo. But here he was in a small basket with a man he hardly knew.

This is it, Harold said. *We could die up here.*

We could die anywhere, Rock said.

Harold's smile landed on Rock's heart. *Do you have any last words for the people below*, Harold asked?

Rock leaned over the side of the basket, carefully, holding Harold's hand. *They're called platypuses, you fuckers*, he yelled and he laughed as he flew away into his one valuable life.

Chris McMahen

Chris McMahen is the author of four novels for young readers including *Box of Shocks*, the winner of the Manitoba Young Readers Choice Award. He is also a past winner of the Okanagan Short Story and Word on the Lake contests. In addition, he has contributed to a number of anthologies.

The Post

Chris McMahen

AT THE BIRCH GROVE RETIREMENT HOME, women outnumbered men eighty-three to one. You could cut the sexual tension with a set of dentures.

At one time, there were as many as five men, but things happened.

Walter Zabotniuk died in the arms of thrice married Hazel Warden– the strain of Hazel's amorous embrace all too much for Walter's heart that burst–most would agree–with happiness.

"One hell of a way to go," quipped Rosalind Parker at bridge the following afternoon. And she meant it in a good way.

Harold Morton went a week later, dropping dead on the spot in Phyllis Cowell's room as he was executing a West Coast Swing move he hadn't done since the war. Phyllis suffered only a sprained wrist, but Harold ruptured something– something vital enough to cause an end to more than just his dancing career.

Donald Morgenson was gone two weeks later–knocked unconscious while attempting to carry Myra Brekaleg through the threshold, just like he had done fifty-seven years earlier with his bride, Elfrieda. Myra was much lighter than Elfrieda, but Donald wasn't quite the man he used to be, so it wasn't entirely surprising that he lost his balance and banged his head on the door jamb. Whether it was the blow to the skull or having Myra land on top of him, it could never be ascertained what the exact cause of death was. Myra walked away unscathed, disconcerted only by the similarity of Donald's unfortunate end to that of her second husband, Abdul.

Xavier Budd died the next day while sharing a dessert with Barbara Ogilvie. He choked on the crust of a slice of cheery pie. Being forever the romantic, he insisted Barbara share his slice of pie and take the fruity section while he would tackle the legendary bulletproof crust.

His choking was quite silent, quite unremarkable, such that the others at his table didn't notice anything unusual. Even when he fell off his chair, this only brought a titter of laughter from Dorothy Markham, Vi Beechly, and Gert Holmstad followed by enthusiastic applause and the cry of, "Bravo!" His hobby as a amateur magician made its way to the dinner table most nights where Xavier would bend forks with his mind, pull scarves out of Cornish game hens, and swallow as many as eight butter knives at one time. And as Xavier keeled over, in the throws of his last gasps, he managed to grab the edge of the table cloth, give it a flick, and fall to the floor with the dirty dishes still left in place on the table. Only after the applause had died did everyone discover that so had Xavier.

That left Al.

Dorothy Markham, Vi Beechly, and Gert Holmstad at table eight had done a ranking of the men who'd lived at Birch Meadows over the past year.

"It's absolutely anonymous," Gert declared, waving her fork with a chunk of meatloaf skewered in the prongs. "That Al character's at the bottom of everyone's list. And that's saying something, considering all the others above him on the list are dead."

They had their reasons for ranking Al below four dead men.

For one, he never came on the retirement home's

outings. And for another, he rarely spoke.

"I've never heard him string more than two words together," Dorothy said, managing to sip her tea with a look of unbroken perplexity.

"Two words? You've heard him say two words?" Gert said, her cup clattering onto her saucer. "I can honestly say I've never heard him utter one single solitary word. I was convinced he was mute. But you say you've heard him speak two words in a row! And what momentous occasion prompted this?"

"Oh, but they were very small words," Dorothy said, shaking her head energetically. "In fact, I don't think they were words at all. They sounded more like grunts. I suppose I was just giving him the benefit of the doubt. Silly me. Always giving people the benefit of the doubt when they really haven't earned it."

"I don't even know his last name," Vi said.

"Last name? Huh!" huffed Ellie Grant who turned her chair around from the table behind. "I don't even really know his first name!"

"Oh, don't tell me that," Dorothy said. "You've seen his name tag."

"Of course I've seen his name tag," Ellie said, rolling her eyes. "But is his real name Alan? Alexander? Albert?

Alfred?"

"Or Alphonzo," Gert said.

"No, he doesn't look like an Alphonzo," Ellie said. "But it could be a shortened version of some foreign name none of us could ever pronounce."

"Like Welsh," Dorothy said.

"Yes! Or another one of those Germanic languages where they always sound like they're about to spit," Ellie said.

"He just might be Welsh. You know how short their ponies are, and he's very short," Gert said. "But you never know. The world is such a strange place these days. I'm glad I'm old."

"Even if he's not Welsh, you have to wonder how he could afford this place," Vi said. "Just look at what he wears. Like he just rolled in from the farm."

In fact, he had.

HAVING BREAKFAST in the dining room with eighty-three women took some getting used to. Prior to last month, Al had spent the previous 18,980 mornings out walking the fence line of his farm a few miles from the Birch Grove Retirement Home. He always told his wife, Lainey, right up until her last days that he was checking the fences, and he supposes he was. But when he was out checking fences, there was no one to tell him anything. There was no gossip, no nagging, no stove-top philosophy. He'd leave the house at 5:00 am and head for the western edge of his land, trudging along, his eyes scanning the barbed wire, then stopping at each post to give it a shake. On he'd walk, his feet landing in the footprints he'd left the previous days as he methodically moved from post to post.

If a post wobbled, he'd pull out a lump of chalk from his back pocket and draw an X near the top, and mumble something about fence posts not being made like they used to. Sometime over the next few days, he'd be back to yank the post from the ground, replacing it with a new one.

By his estimation, over the years he'd been running the farm, he'd replaced each and every post along his fence line at least three times. Except for one.

At the far corner of his property where his hay field bordered Jigs McGregor's field of sunflowers was a post Al had sunk it into the ground in 1959– the year he took over the farm from Lainey's old man. Every day, he'd approach it, stop and look it up and down, then cup his hand over the top and give it a shake. It never budged. It was as solid as the day it was driven into the ground.

He told Lainey it was a miracle of sorts, but she said God doesn't use up miracles on fence posts. Al wasn't a spiritual man, but that post always made him wonder. "What the hell?" he'd mumble each morning after giving it his customary shake. "If there ever was a miracle, it's this post," he'd say looking skyward. His mother had told him that the only thing in this world you could rely on was God. But now, Al knew better. There was God and this post.

THE MORNING HIS SON, Grange, and his wife pulled away from the farmhouse in the van with Al and a suitcase in the back seat, headed for the Birch Grove Retirement Home, they had to pull over for the bulldozer. Al was thinking of the new roof he'd put on three years ago, and the new wallpaper in the bathroom that went up just before Lainey went. And there were those new energy efficient widows just last fall. But bulldozers weren't conducive to salvaging. They have a job to do and new wallpaper's just not part of the equation.

Grange first brought up the idea of the golf course when he drove Al to the hospital to visit Lainey. He mentioned it again when they were in the waiting room at the funeral home trying to decide on the model of casket. The third time was when he was helping Al with his tie just before the funeral. Each time, Grange prefaced his argument with, "I know it might not seem like the best time to bring this up . . ." And each time, Al's only reply was a wave of his hand as if he was batting away an irritating fly.

But it was different the fourth time around. They were sitting in the living room wrapped in quilts and wearing their winter coats while they waited for Fergy's Home Heating to show up and revive the furnace. Grange used no preface, and Al had no flies to swat. He just said, "Okay. I may as well give it a try."

Grange went on and on about how the timing was perfect and the golf course was a no-risk investment being part of a bomb proof growth industry, and on and on. But Grange was talking to himself. While he talked, Al questioned his own unusual spontaneity. He usually slept on decisions– like when he bought the new pick-up back in '83. Or when he decided to buy that herd of bison from Ray Wallace from down the road. But the Ford pickup was a lemon, and the bison didn't work out, so in the back of his mind, he knew that sleeping on a decision didn't make one whiff of difference. He'd been pretty spontaneous when he proposed to Lainey– so spontaneous, he doesn't even remember doing it. She swore he went down on one knee, but back then, that might have had more to do with a bottle of rye than any romantic notion. Anyway, whatever did happen, things worked out alright. And he hoped this move to the luxury of the retirement home might work out just as well.

And maybe it was finally time to move on. The farm hadn't changed in fifty years, but he had. He'd danced around the annual cycle of plough, plant, harvest, breed, fatten slaughter. But every year, the dance took just a bit more effort than the year before. First, it was his knees that gave him trouble, then it was his back. The last few years, it was the arthritis in his hands.

Al knew there would eventually be some sort of end– a cliff or a wall– some sort of definitive end when his walk around the fence line would be his last. He figured something might happen, and he wouldn't have a choice. The end would come, and that would be that. But that's not the way it went. Grange asked Al to make a decision. It was like putting the dog down. It's easy if it just crawls off and dies somewhere, but when you have to decide, that's the killer.

But Grange caught him at a good time or bad time– Al wasn't sure which– and he gave in. Within a week, Grange and his wife came by to pick him up and take him to the Birch Grove Retirement Home. "You'll absolutely love the place," Marlene said, tugging at the pompoms on the back of her golf socks. "After your hard life, you deserve a bit of luxury," she said, then winked.

Al had never considered his life "hard." But he'd never thought it was easy, either. He just didn't think in those terms. His life just was.

Eight miles later, Grange stopped the van and Marlene patted him on the knee. "Well, here we are! Awesome luxury. Just awesome," Marlene said, holding his arm as he climbed out of the van, down onto the yellow bricks of the entryway.

ELLIE, GERT AND DOROTHY usually hurried through breakfast on Thursdays– no marmalade on their toast, no second cup of decaf, no idle chit-chat. For they knew as they ate, Annika, the perky activities co-ordinator at Birch Grove, was posting the sign-up sheets on the bulletin board outside the card room for the next week's outings. This week, there was a trip to the Prune Plum Mall, a picnic to Otter Lake Park, and a visit to

Maxwells' Orchards. It was first come first served for the sign-up with only twenty seats on the bus. With a few gulps, the last bites of dry toast were washed down, and they were off. Dorothy had a walker, so she'd lead the way, using her hardware to gain position if a line-up had already formed.

This morning, they were lucky. There was only one person ahead of them. It was Al.

"Thank God I re-polidented this morning," Dorothy said. "Otherwise, I would have lost my dentures for sure!"

"I thought I'd seen everything," Ellie said.

"It doesn't get any stranger than this," Gert added.

They all stood back and watched Al finish writing his name, then stand and gaze at the paper. Finally, he let the pencil drop so it dangled on the end of a string, turned and headed past the women, his head down, shuffling off to his room.

Dorothy pushed past the others and lunged at the dangling pencil. She fumbled with her glasses that hung from a silver chain around her neck.

"Oh, my God," she said. "He's actually signed up for a trip."

"To where? The mall?" Ellie said, pushing closer.

"No. It's to a farm. A fruit farm called Maxwells' Orchards."

"Goodness knows why he'd want to go to an orchard," Gert said.

"Strange. Very strange," Dorothy said, as she wrote her name two spaces below Al's.

"Very strange, indeed," Ellie said, snatching the pencil out of Dorothy's hand.

THE BUS WAS SCHEDULED to leave at 1:30. When Carl, the driver, arrived to get the bus ready, he opened the door and found Al already on the bus sitting on the seat right behind the driver's.

As Carl climbed onto the bus, he said, "You're an eager beaver. Can't wait to escape this place, eh?"

Al dug around in his pocket and pulled out a fistful of crumpled bills. He tried to speak, but his voice cracked. Then, he cleared his throat and said, "Please take this as a compliment, but you are the first person I've ever bribed in my life."

They were late leaving. It was nearly 2:00 by the time everyone was in their seats and the walkers were loaded in the storage compartment.

Dorothy, Ellie and Gert managed to squeeze onto

the seat right behind Al who sat alone, his back ramrod straight, his hands cupping the knees of his fortrel slacks. As the bus pulled out onto the street, he looked straight ahead, never glancing from side to side.

Dorothy nudged Ellie and gave her a knowing nod, but Ellie had no idea what she meant or what she was referring to. Ellie nodded back knowingly anyway, continuing their non-verbal miscommunication.

Houses started thinning out as they reached the city limits. Al leaned back, heaving a few deep breaths as his shoulders sagged and the creases in his forehead relaxed, his eyes blinking more slowly.

"Just look for the barn with the sagging roof up ahead," he said, leaning toward Carl. "It's the first right after that."

The bus slowed, and Carl turned up a gravel road. "I hope you know I could get fired for this," he said, smiling.

"It's okay, Carl," Al replied. "My son's a good lawyer."

The bus rattled along, crossing washboard, ducking into potholes.

Dorothy leaned toward Ellie and stage whispered, "Something just isn't right, here, Ellie. I feel it in my bones. Something just isn't right."

"Actually, I'm finding this rather exciting," Ellie replied. "Like a little adventure."

On both sides of the road, rolling fields stretched onward, punctuated by the odd farmhouse and out building.

"Slow her down, Carl. It's just up here on the right at the top of the hill," Al said, leaning far enough forward so he was nearly standing.

Carl pulled the bus over and stopped, pulling the double doors open.

"This doesn't look much like an orchard to me," Dorothy said. "If this is an orchard, this is the worst outing I've ever taken in all my days!"

"Just sit tight, everyone. We won't be a minute," Carl said over the P.A. on the bus, the first time he'd ever used it.

Al pulled himself up off the edge of the seat and gingerly took the stairs sideways, his arms shaking as he held the handrail. Carl got up to help, but Al waved him away. "Now, you just sit tight and make sure none of those other old bods don't do anything foolish," Al said.

"What in God's name is he doing?" Dorothy said.

"He's just got a bit of business to attend to," Carl

said. "Don't you worry. He won't be long."

Off the final step, Al stumbled as he stepped onto the gravel, but a quick hop got him back in balance. He stepped off the gravel road and waded into a field of sunflowers, parting the stalks with his arms as he went.

"You don't go too far, there, Mr. Godfrey!" Carl called. He was out of his seat, crouching down to see out the bus, watching Al swim his way into the sunflowers.

Everyone watched as Al move further and further from the road, disappearing into the sunflowers. For a while, they could follow his progress by the swaying of the sunflowers, but eventually, they couldn't see anything at all.

"Holy shit!" Carl said under his breath as he leapt off the bus and plunged into the field, thrashing his way through the sunflowers. But in the tall stalks, it was easy to become disoriented. After a few minutes, Carl shouted, "Where the hell are you?" before stumbling out of the sunflowers and onto the road about fifty yards away from the bus. He jogged back along the road, then broke into a run. "What the hell?" he shouted.

The bus was empty. From the edge of the road, he could see a path trampled through the sunflowers. He ran along, following the bent stalks through the field.

"They couldn't have gone far," he said, his run slowing to a jog as he wheezed and coughed, his shirt soaked with perspiration.

The path of trampled sunflowers wound its way through the field, curving, bending, correcting, climbing up a rise. And when he reached the crest of a hill, he looked down. There they were. They all stood at the bottom of the hill where the field of sunflowers ended at a fence line.

The field beyond the fence was a mess of churned soil, lines of plastic piping spreading in every direction, and a lifeless bulldozer sitting not five feet from the edge of the sunflowers.

They stood at the edge of the field in a semi-circle, no one making a move, their heads bowed as if in prayer. When Carl reached them, he realized their heads weren't bent in prayer. They were staring down at the ground. He pushed his way past Dorothy and Ellie, and there was Al. He lay face down on the ground, his arms wrapped around a broken off old fence post pinned beneath him.

"It looks like he didn't see it coming," Ellie said.

Carl rolled Al onto his back and tried to administer C.P.R., but it was too late.

"Just like all the other men," Dorothy said, "I knew he was no different from the rest."

Shawn L. Bird

Shawn L. Bird is an author and poet in the beautiful Shuswap region of BC where her miniature poodle and responsible husband keep her busy. Her *Murdering Mr. Edwards* was nominated for an Arthur Ellis Crime Writing Award in the novella category. You can visit her website at ShawnBird.com

Consternation, Constancy, & Constantinople
or
The Diminutive Dilemma

Shawn L. Bird

"HELLO. I'M CYBIL. We're going to Turkey," the little girl told the man as he re-arranged his suitcase and hat on the rack above their heads in the train compartment. "We're going to meet my Grandmama Benza."

An umbrella fell out of the rack; the man caught it mid-air.

"Oh! Mama's parasol!" said Cybil. "You're lucky it didn't land on your head."

"Indeed," said the man as he tucked the parasol back on the rack. The man was not fond of children, but she stared up at him with such endearingly huge dark eyes that he found himself smiling as he settled on the seat across from her in the train compartment. There was a small boy sitting silently beside her. "Turkey, you

35

say? That's a long trip." He hoped he'd be able to change compartments. Children were inevitably trouble.

"I know. Mama says it's far too long for children to be without a nanny and that we're going to drive her mad. Right, Hector?"

A tiny, solemn little boy sitting on her other side nodded. "Mad," he murmured and then looked out the window. Puffs of steam from the engine floated by as the rails clicked beneath them.

"Where *is* your mother?" the man said. They were awfully small to be left by themselves, weren't they? He had no experience of child travellers, though the girl seemed competent enough.

Cybil sat up a bit straighter, pursed her lips, and said demurely, "She needed the *facilities*." She gazed down at the ground when she said 'facilities' so as not to embarrass anyone.

"Ah," said the man, feeling somewhat chastened. "Has she been gone long?" He'd been in the compartment a good ten minutes already. Had he seen a motherly woman in the corridor of any of the carriages as he'd been searching for space in a compartment?

"No," said the girl with a toss of her curls. "She's not been gone long, has she Hector?"

"Not long," he replied, without looking away from the countryside passing the window.

"I see," said the man, thinking again of the people he'd passed as he made his way along the corridor and dismissing them one by one. "You're sure?"

Cybil chortled a strangely grown up laugh. "Of course, I'm sure. Ladies always take a long time in the facilities." She leaned forward and whispered conspiratorally, "It's all the petticoats. They are frightful to manage without a maid. And Mama would not bring a maid. Right, Hector?"

"Couldn't," said Hector without a backward's glance. He pulled a piece of paper out of his pocket and read it, silently mouthing the words.

Cybil sighed dramatically, "Couldn't. Just so."

The man raised an inquisitive eyebrow, but Cybil didn't respond, and he didn't want to probe. In any case, it wasn't too difficult to imagine a situation in which a mother would be taking children to their grandmother without a maid or nanny. Likely *reduced circumstances*, as they say. How sad.

"Would you like to see Hector's caravan?"

"I beg your pardon?" said the man.

"Hector has a lovely caravan. Inside is a lovely

stove, and a tiny kettle, and a bed with a counterpane. It's pulled by the most wonderful calico horse."

"A calico horse?" said the man, completely unable to imagine such a creature. "You mean one coloured like a calico cat? White, black, and orange?"

"No silly!" Cybil laughed. "With little flowers!"

The man blinked at her, trying to see how this could be possible.

Hector looked away from the window, "You're not to touch my caravan. You promised. Melvin gave it to *me*."

"But it's ever so lovely!" said Cybil plaintively.

"No," said Hector. "It's in my case and it's staying in the case until I take it out." He looked over to the man. "I put a lock on the case. She doesn't have the key." Then he turned away again, and stared determinedly out the window, muttering what sounded like a nonsense rhyme.

Cybil pursed her lips and leaned back into the seat, her nostrils twitching, but she didn't say a word. The man thought her nanny had done a very good job of teaching her to contain a tantrum. Or was it the elusive mother?

Finally, Cybil reached under her seat and pulled up

a basket. She took a book from a pocket in the lining along the edge. "If you'll excuse me," she said with a flick of her eyes to her brother who glanced at her, "I'll just read for a while."

The man nodded, "Of course. An excellent plan. I think I will do so, as well. He pulled his own book from within the pocket of his coat and flipped through the pages in search of his bookmark.

Cybil's eyes grew large. She met her brother's eyes and tipped her head meaningfully.

Hector nodded.

The man, focused on the pages of his book, didn't notice their silent communication.

He read.

Cybil read.

Hector looked out the window.

In the silence, the man thought he could hear an odd noise beyond the clacking of the train. It was like the scratching of a mouse trapped in box. Undoubtedly there were many rodents travelling in the walls or seats of the carriages. It would be wiser not to draw it to the children's attention if there was one in this compartment. Didn't girls shriek and leap onto things when in the vicinity of rodents?

Eventually, the man's stomach began to growl.

The girl giggled and caught her brother's eye. Hector smirked.

The man coughed his embarrassment. He folded his book, tucked it into the coat, and then reached toward the door.

"Where are you going?" asked Cybil.

The man cleared his throat. "I just need to stretch my legs."

"You can stretch your legs in here!" She demonstrated by lifting one leg and then the other, wafting the lace on her frilly ankle socks.

"Maybe," said Hector, "he has manly things to do, and he doesn't want to discuss them with a nosy girl."

Cybil sniffed.

"I'll keep an eye out for your mother while I'm in the corridor. What is her name?"

"Mama," said Cybil.

Hector snorted. "He means the name grown-ups call her, silly."

Cybil scowled at him.

Hector said, "She's usually called Mrs. Montague-Smythe."

"Usually?" said the man.

Hector shrugged.

"Sometimes, she's called *Mama*," said Cybil with a glare at Hector.

The man nodded, "Oh, of course. Perhaps Mrs. Montague-Smythe will be here upon my return. I will be gone some time. I think I'll stop in the dining carriage and have dinner." He stepped into the corridor. He would look for the porter and report these odd motherless children. He had no intention of becoming responsible for them just because he shared a compartment with them.

Cybil waited until she heard the carriage door close behind him. "Well, what do you think? Will he do?"

Hector shrugged. "He seems boring."

"Boring is just what we need," she hissed. "No one notices boring. If mother were more boring we wouldn't be in this predicament, would we?"

"We're in this predicament because of Marvelous Melvin the Magnificent. Don't blame mother."

"She didn't have to volunteer."

"Of course, she did. Melvin said if she volunteered he'd give her twenty pounds. We needed twenty pounds. Trips to Turkey are expensive!"

There was scratching from beneath their seat.

Hector swung his feet, thudding into the case stowed there, and the noise stopped.

"It's a good thing she'd already bought the train tickets, and that I was holding her reticule, that's all I can say."

"I wish," Hector sighed.

"You wish what?"

"I wish that's all you would say. But I bet it isn't."

"Don't be rude."

"Don't you." Hector looked back out the window and then sighed. "This doesn't help. We have a decision to make."

"I think he'll do."

"Maybe someone better will get on at the next stop."

"It'll be harder if there are two adults in the compartment. You can see he's already suspicious. What if he talks to the porter? I say we do it when he gets back. Perhaps he'll take a nap. Come on, Hector. You know we have to do it soon."

"I'm hungry," said Hector. "We should go to the dining car. I'm sure someone will feel sorry for us and buy us a meal."

"We can't draw any attention like that, you know that. We have bread and butter for today, anyway." She rummaged in her basket and handed him bread wrapped in butcher paper. "We can go to the dining car tomorrow."

Hector considered. "I guess we'll have more money tomorrow, too. Did you see, when he took out his book, his wallet was bulging so much it hardly fit in his breast pocket!"

"I saw."

"Should I get my case out now?"

Cybil watched the trees and fields outside the window. "Not quite yet. Perhaps be on your hands and knees when he comes back." She stood on the seat and brought down Mama's parasol.

Hector wrinkled his brows as he watched her and then he laughed. "Oh! I see what you mean to do. Excellent plan!"

"Thank you." Cybil settled back into her seat feeling rather proud of herself. She liked it when Hector admitted she had good ideas. So far, they were even. Hector had had a good idea while Marvelous Melvin was huffling and apologizing, wimpering and assuring them that this had never happened before. Cybil had had a good idea to get on the train. If this plan worked, she'd be winning: two good ideas to one.

They heard the door to the carriage open with the loud clattering of rails, Cybil peeked out the compartment window and nodded to Hector. "Now!"

Hector dropped to the floor, on his hands and knees. His head was at the seat; his buttocks protruded across the threshold.

Comfortably satiated and feeling confident the porter would be along shortly, the man stepped inside their compartment and promptly tripped over Hector's small body. "Oof!" he grunted as he stumbled.

With remarkable coordination, Hector kicked out a foot to slam the door closed and then rolled tight against the seats while Cybil brought down the parasol with all the power she possessed. With a crack, the parasol made contact where she aimed: the niche where neck meets skull. The man flopped onto the floor precisely where Hector had been a moment before.

"Good thinking to roll out of the way," said Cybil, slightly annoyed that now their good ideas were tied again.

Hector poked at the man with his toe. "I suddenly imagined what I'd look like squished as flat as a bug on the window." He looked between the man and the case under his seat. "How am I supposed to get my case out now? He's in the way."

They pushed and tugged until the man was wedged with his back against the seat, legs out straight in front of him, his head lolling onto his chest.

"The porter will know something is wrong if he sees him like this when he comes to make up the berths," said Hector.

"So hurry up about it!" said Cybil. "Get it out."

Hector had worked hard to wedge his case under the seat when they'd arrived in the compartment, and it took some effort to get it out again. There was a sheen of perspiration across his forehead when he finally dropped onto his seat with his case on his lap.

The scratching and squeaking had started up again. Hector gave the case a little shake and it stopped again.

"Are you sure you can remember what to say?"

Hector rolled his eyes. He pulled the paper from his pocket. "I've been practising."

"Maybe it won't work."

"Maybe it won't." He shrugged.

Cybil furrowed her brows. "What will we do, if it doesn't?"

"We'll wait until he comes around and tell him your parasol hit him after he tripped over me." He stared at

45

her earnestly. "In other words, exactly what *did* happen."

"Oh, yes," said Cybil frowning. "Of course." Hector was now up three good ideas to her two. "Hurry up."

"Close your eyes while I get the key."

Cybil obliged, though she knew very well the key was on a string around his neck, tucked inside his shirt.

"All right. You can open them." Hector had unlocked the case. The key was beside him on the seat. With great care, he removed his remarkable caravan and its delightful calico horse from the case. He closed the case and set the caravan on top so they could admire it. It was a traditional Romani style caravan, painted in bright red with yellow and blue swirls and flowers. A little stove pipe stuck out the top. As they watched, a puff of smoke wafted into the air. Free from its harness was the lovely daffodil yellow horse painted in red and white flowers. Hector set it down beside him on the seat. It shook its mane and flicked its tail.

Cybil sighed. "Can I hold it?"

"Take it then," said Hector. "I need to concentrate."

As Cybil reached across the compartment to gently gather the horse onto her hand, a face appeared at the tiny window.

"Hello, Mama," said Hector.

His mother, presently only five inches tall, was gesticulating and squeaking wildly. She was wearing her long grey skirt and white blouse. She'd taken off her travelling jacket and her lovely hat with the cabbage roses.

"We can't understand you, Mama," said Cybil. "But we're going to try to fix things. Hector learned the words from Marvelous Melvin."

Hector opened the caravan door. His mother walked out onto his hand. He set her beside him on the seat. He arranged the man's hand on the caravan. "Do you have it?" he asked Cybil. He rummaged in his pocket for the paper where he'd written down the spell.

Cybil nodded and opened her parasol. Cello taped to the shaft was the wand she had stolen from Marvelous Melvin the Magnificent at the magic show where so much had gone horribly wrong. She handed it to Hector and closed her eyes tightly, just as she had at the magic show.

Suddenly she cried, "Stop!"

Mama and Hector stared at her. "Mama! You need your jacket and hat! Imagine travelling without them!"

Mama gasped and jumped up, running to Hector's

hand. He set her at the caravan door.

Meanwhile, Cybil pulled the bulging wallet out of the man's coat. "Here," she said. "We'll need this."

Mama emerged from the caravan in her full finery, pinning her hat in place. Hector smiled as he set her beside him on the seat. His mama was very elegant standing there like a fashionable figurine, looking around the compartment.

"Better sit down, Mama," said Cybil. "You don't want to bump your head."

Their Mama, sometimes also known as Mrs. Elizabeth Marie Ellen Montague-Smythe settled onto her bottom and wiggled forward until her feet were tangled in the man's slightly greasy hair.

Hector read the words on the paper over again. He held the wand tightly. He glanced to his mother and down at the man. He took a deep breath. He lifted the wand, and with a swish and flick he said the words.

Sparks dripped from the wand and fell onto the man.

The man groaned. His eyes twitched.

But that was all.

Cybil leaned forward and glared at Hector. "You have to say it like you *mean* it!"

Hector narrowed his eyes and stared at the man. He looked between his mother and Cybil. He straightened his shoulders, gripped the wand tightly, then he swished and flicked purposely as he spoke the nonsense words with all the authority he could muster.

Light exploded in the compartment.

"Well," said Mrs. Montague-Smythe sitting full size on the seat beside her son, "this is a considerable improvement. Thank you." With her toe, she nudged the tiny man sitting on the floor of the compartment. He flopped over onto his side like a doll. "You'd better put this in the caravan, Cybil."

Cybil picked the tiny man up and studied him. He made a funny doll. She gave him a little shake, hoping he'd wake up. When he didn't, Cybil put the man into the caravan and then she set the caravan and the calico horse into Hector's case. Hector gave her the wallet, and she pushed it in, too.

Hector turned the lock and pushed the case back under his seat.

"Darlings," said Mama, "I am very proud of your clear thinking and determination. Melvin was a menace. You two are the real magical marvels!"

Hector and Cybil grinned at each other. "Thank you,

Mama," they said in perfect chorus.

Mama looked out the window at the scenery passing by. "It will be so lovely to see your Grandmama Benza," she sighed. "She'll be able to fix all these little problems. Family is so much better together."

"Like us!" said Cybil.

Mama nodded. "Indeed, darling girl. Sometimes it's hard work to keep a family together, I'm so glad we have each other."

Hector smiled up at her, and she wrapped her arm around him and gave him an affectionate squeeze.

A firm knocking sounded on the door, "Porter!" said a man in a navy uniform gleaming with shining brass buttons as he opened the door.

"Good evening," said Mrs. Montague-Smythe, smiling beatifically at him. She rose to her feet. "I'm glad to see you. We're just on our way to dinner. Please set up the sleeping berths."

"Oh!" said the porter. "Who are you?"

Cybil said, "She's mama, of course."

"Ah," said the porter. "Of course. And Mr. Harrison?"

"I don't know any Mr. Harrison," said Mama. "Let's go, darlings."

If the porter heard any squeaking while he set up the sleeping berths, he didn't pay it any mind.

Janet L Whitehead

Janet is best known as an advocate for the creative soul, helping others to finish their creative projects. Sometimes she gets to her own projects, though, including the anthology *Writerly Curiosities* and her creative memoir *Beyond All Imaginings*. Her creative works: Musingsandmud.com and Novelminds.ca

Searching for Weedlings

Janet L Whitehead

"I HAVE A BEER AND A TALE TO TELL!" Derek announced as he got out of his truck and sauntered to the porch.

"I heard a story from a woman who is a friend of an old guy whose friend had a sister who had a bizarre but kind of magical incident when she was four," Derek said as he settled into the old adirondack chair.

"Oh, I'm sure it's true, then." Lily's smirk said otherwise. Still, she, too, settled into her chair, grabbing his beer for a quick sip. He was the one person she found agreeable in her solitary life. Two old fogies on a porch telling stories. He did all the talking, though.

"Pfft. I'm telling you this story because you like magical things. Smart ass." Derek responded.

"Seems like you had to do some digging to get this one," Lilly laughed.

"No, no. An odd old lady told me. Way older than us. She's been hanging about in town for a while. She called me over at the pub. Said 'I hear you're a storyteller. I've got one for you.' You gotta know that intrigued me," Derek laughed, "But it's a good story. True, I think. Pretty sad, though. Still, there's magic, so just listen...

I remember exactly how she started the story. Because I had to look up crinoline. In case that had something to do with the magical part. It doesn't, though. I don't think. But, anyway, this little girl, the four-year-old, was dressed up in a fancy white crinoline dress. The kind with fuzzy roses, I was told. She loved the little fuzzy roses and rubbed her tiny fingers on them as she walked in the field."

"Well, that part is true, at least. Little girls loved those dresses," Lily said, petting her old collie and crooning, "Yes, little girls loved those dresses, didn't they."

Derek reached over and gave the dog an ear scratch, "Such a good boy. Anyway, the old guy's friend told the woman's friend that the brother said his little sister was looking for weedlings. 'Weedlings!' thought the little girl. The family was camping, but only for a place to stay because they were going to a wedding in the nearby town. The little girl was dressed in her best dress. Her mom told her to keep her dress clean while she got her brothers ready. But she was four and she went in search of the weedlings. It makes sense, right? She's four, looking for a misheard weedling and she was going to show her big brothers how smart she was by finding the weedlings all by herself."

"She has big brothers? How do you know that?" Lily asked.

"Obviously she has at least one brother who shared the story. But there's two in the story. Just listen... The little girl wasn't sure what a weedling might be until... along the edge of the lake (there was a lake, by the way) there were tall reeds with puff balls on top. 'Those must be weedlings,' thought the girl, 'Pretty!'

The little girl stepped down the soft bank of grass and reached for a weedling puff. As she did, the bank slid away and she slid with it into the lake. She couldn't swim and panicked trying to grab at the bank, but the dirt just kept pulling away."

"So, this is gonna be a short story, then, is it?" snickered Lily.

"Lily, it's a cool story! Shut up and listen!" Derek

continued, "The little girl kicked her feet but her head went under anyway. She grabbed at a weedling and pulled herself up, yelling out for help.

Standing right there, laughing, if you can imagine, was her brother! Now there's a reason for this but right then and there, the little girl was certain her brother was going to just let her drown. The dirt kept pulling away. The water was cold. Her dress was going to be ruined. Her mom would be mad. And she was going to die."

"Wait. Why would the storyteller know all that? The kid lived to tell the tale?" Lily shifted to the edge of her seat, intrigued.

"Kind of. She gave up on grabbing the bank and kicked, sputtering and splashing, to reach some of those... you know, those wide leaf plant things in water..."

"Lily pads?" Lily asked.

"Ha ha, ya, I guess with a name like yours you'd know what they are. So, she grabbed at the lily pads and her feet grabbed at the roots of the plant underwater and she had a split second of thinking she'd be okay. A split second to gasp for a breath, when she saw her other brother also laughing at her. She started sinking again in the murky green water. She remembered that part, you know -the murky green water full of weeds and yellow pollen."

"Pretty smart for kid to know it was pollen. But, of course, you heard this from a friend of a friend of a friend, bla bla, whose friend had a sister. Kind of sounds like an urban myth. And you say it's magical? This is a bit silly," Lily raised an eyebrow at her old friend.

"Well, that's just it. They said it was pollen. But the little girl said otherwise. So, the old lady said the story told from the girl's brother was that his sister – I think her name was Laura or something – saw sparkles, not pollen. Sparkles like gold glitter, the little girl said. You know, after she was saved.

Nobody believed her. Her brothers told an entirely different story. But for her, she saw gold sparkles. And those gold sparkles, she said, turned into bluish little lights and ... well, then, she flapped her arms to surface and get some air, before flailing once again like she was being dragged under and couldn't stop it."

"Derek, I never knew you were this great of a storyteller!"

"Just telling it like I heard it," Derek answered.

"Uh, huh. Sure," Lily mocked.

"Do you want to hear this story or not?"

"Yeah, I'm sorry. It's just quite ... I dunno. Do go on," Lily squirmed in the porch chair, eyes darting around the yard, twirling her gray hair.

"Okay. You're being weird."

"No, no, just wondering where the cat is. Oh, here she is," Lily gave her knee a pat, and the Persian easily leaped up and curled onto her lap.

"Anyway," Derek leaned forward in his chair, capturing Lily's eyes so she had to pay attention. "This time the little girl went under and couldn't get back to the surface for air. She was under for far too long. Her brothers finally realized this was no joke and slid down the bank to save their sister. The water was shallow, barely past their knees and that's why they'd been laughing. They knew their sister just had to stand up and they figured she would. The boys splashed their arms through the water to reach her but she wasn't there.

The little girl, though, she was there. She told everyone later that the bluish lights pulled together into a shape. She couldn't breathe, but it didn't matter, she could smile. The shape was, at first, a duck. And then the little girl laughed, even under water, when the duck became all furry, with the sweetest puppy dog eyes. A puppy with a giant bill, smiling at her, swirling its body around her. The creature nudged her under her bottom to push her to the surface, but she slipped off giggling. (She was giggling, Lily, under water!) Shimmering lights swirled with the creature and then she saw the creature had added a giant tail. Like a beaver, she told people later. The iridescent creature slapped its tail and a shower of golden glitter surrounded her once again. She heard a whisper say, 'You will need this magic.' She grasped the creature's tail and was flipped high into the air, landing with a splash nearly into her brother's arms. She was laughing! And, here's weird, she kind of had her own iridescent glow about her."

Lily tucked her knees into her long skirt, pulled her sweater tight around her shoulders and, looking down as she pet the dog, she said, "Well, was she okay then?"

"No, not really. She told everyone her story in her four year old way. At six, she told it again, trying hard for people to understand. And she kept trying as she grew older. But, her brother said, it was pretty hard to believe and he had no idea what had really happened. The thing was, once in a while she would glow. The family figured the pollen had affected her skin somehow. And when she was still quite young, she did

59

strange things. She suddenly could dive into the water, swim below the surface for far too long, and come to the surface laughing. Her mom joked that she was having a playdate with her magical creature friend. When she learned at school that there was such a thing as a platypus, she raced home to tell her family it was a platypus that saved her. 'Honey, you live in British Columbia,' her mom said, 'there's no platypuses here.' 'But, it's a magic platypus,' the little girl sighed.

And you know how kids can be, all the kids teased her. They teased her when she glowed. They called her a liar. Kids are awful sometimes, aren't they? Even the adults in town thought she was weird. The little girl did have her pets to comfort her, her brother told the old guy who told the friend of the old woman's friend. She loved dogs, cats, squirrels, and birds, and they loved her. Maybe it was these animals that kept her okay for a while. But, I guess, not happy enough. She was about 12 when she gave her mom a big hug and took her pets down for a swim. But, this time she never came back. Neither did the animals. The whole town searched for the little girl for days, months, even years. Her brother said everyone was ashamed, including himself, for teasing the little girl for so long. They knew they had driven her to her demise. Pretty sad tale, after all." Derek sighed, "But magical, right?"

"Right," Lily said, as she stood up and headed down the steps. The cat and dog followed.

"Oh, and wait, if you think this story isn't true, the old lady said she heard there was a beautiful statue erected in the little girl's honour. A statue of the girl, surrounded by animals, including one platypus. A magical platypus, the old woman said. That'd be cool, wouldn't it? To find that town? To go see if the statue really exists?"

"I don't think so," Lily answered, as she started down the path to the lake. "It's hot. I'm going for a swim."

"Lily, wouldn't it be fun to go on a little adventure together? You never leave this place."

But then he saw it. As Lily hiked her skirt up to step around a rock. A glow. Her leg. And her hand, too.

"Laura!" he called.

She turned to face him, mouth open. Her face was iridescent.

"Laura, it's you, isn't it? Oh, wow. It's you. What the hell. The old woman said I needed to know this story. Laura, it's you!"

"My name is Lily now," she said. She turned and hastily headed towards the lake, her loyal animals by her side.

"Wait! I know the story is true," Derek called out to her, "I believe you. I know the whole story is true. I knew it the moment I heard it. Stop, Lily!"

He tried to follow her, but his feet wouldn't move past the deck. Blue and gold dust circled his feet like weights.

"Oh my god, Lily! Don't leave. Don't run away! You know I've always said you were magical, right? I meant it. I love that you are. Come back. I can keep your secret. Or we can share it together with the world. Whatever you want. Don't leave me, Lily," Derek's voice broke, desperate to stop her. He heard a voice whisper, 'Tell her the truth.'

"Lily, I've always loved you!" Derek yelled.

Lily paused. Her eyes teared up. She felt it, too. For the first time in decades, she felt love for another person. The dog and the cat looked up at her, waiting for her next move. They leaped in anticipation as she took that first step back towards Derek. But then she paused. The animals paused.

Derek frantically tried to move his feet, calling to

her, but he was stuck. He held his breath when he saw Lily take that next step. And another. And then, she raced towards Derek, the animals getting there first and circling him playfully. Whatever was holding him back stopped. He stumbled down the steps, arms wide as Lily leaped into the first hug she had had in decades.

Derek kissed her head with a sob. "You're safe now, Lily. You're safe."

Lily lifted her head to look at him, waiting for the horror, or the laughter, or the quick glance away, when he saw her glow up close.

"My god, you are beautiful," he whispered. His hand touched her cheek.

Lily sobbed into his shoulder, unable to speak through the tears. She hugged Derek tighter, melting into a new kind of joy she did not remember ever feeling, and glowing brighter than she had ever glowed before.

The hug, however, was disrupted by a great splash in the lake.

"What the...?" Derek stiffened, listening for more.

"It's okay," Lily laughed, "He's gotten pretty big now. Apparently, he wants to meet you!"

"Um... sure. Sure! I'm all in," Derek grinned.

In all of this loving commotion, they missed one thing. They did not see the dog and the cat nod to the ancient woman standing in a bush not so far away. Perhaps one day, someone will tell someone else's friend who will tell someone who is somehow connected to this story, about the whole role the odd old woman played. Probably not, though, unless the Collie and the Persian cat decide to talk.

You're invited to check out
these other books
from Lintusen Press!

HEAVENS TO MURGATROYD:

stories & poems

A collection of stories that all include a character called Murgatroyd, as a metaphor for strength and creativity.

Includes work from authors Shawn L. Bird, Laurène Boutin, Finnian Burnett, Sherry Cassells, Renee Cronley, Susan Duffield-Lodge, Robyn Diner, Lindsey Harrington,Trevor Hodges, Zilla Jones, Alma Lee, Lavinia Leon, Trent Lewin, Tom McCann, Robert Runté, Donnalynn Rainey, Janet Richards, M. Gail Stelter, and T.L. Tomljanovic.

GHOSTLY

13 tales from beyond the veil

A collection of haunting short stories from Alix Kelinda, Finnian Burnett, Halli Reid, Jarrod K Williams, Jeanna Mason Stay, Kaitlyn Petry, L. N. Hunter, Lee F. Patrick, Leslie Wibberley, Marie Powell, Rob Nisbet, Shawn L. Bird, and Theric Jepson.

THE DRAGON PROBLEM
a collaborative novel

The village of Zos has a dragon problem.
Follow the townsfolk as they deal with an evil dentist, a decrepit dragon, a musical milkmaid, and political shenanigans.

A roomful of authors brainstormed this novel at When Words Collide Writers' Conference in 2023 and 10 authors worked together in subsequent months to craft this entertaining tale.

NEW SPACES:
an anthology of sci-fi short stories

Within your mind and across the universe,
are new spaces to explore!

From Lintusen Press comes this collection of ten science
fiction short stories from authors Finnian Burnett,
Andrew G. Cooper, J. Paul Cooper, BC Deeks, Nancy
Kilpatrick, Philip Mann, Lee F. Patrick, Halli Reid, KT
Wagner, and Jarrod K. Williams.

SMALL SHIFTS:
short stories of fantastical transformation

Not all shifters turn into magnificent beasts. Sure, there are those humans who transform into wolves and bears, but this book is about the smaller creatures. Learn about the trials and tribulations of folks who turn into raccoons, hamsters, mosquitoes, or bumblebees. 11 delightful tales of Small Shifts.

THE DRABBLE ADVENT CALENDAR

A drabble is a story of precisely one hundred words. Here are 25 family friendly winter themed drabbles; one perfectly complete tidbit of story to savour each day leading up to Christmas from authors Carol Parchewsky, Chris McMahen, Finnian Burnett, Lee F. Patrick, Shawn L. Bird, and Tim Reynolds.

Please visit

LintusenPress.ca

to learn more about our upcoming releases

and to see submission calls

for our future publications.

Thank you for leaving a review

on your favourite site or retailer

if you enjoyed this book.